A Little Princess

A novelization by Diane Molleson
Based on the
Screenplay by Richard LaGravenese and Elizabeth Chandler
From the book by Frances Hodgson Burnett

SCHOLASTIC INC.
New York Toronto London Auckland Sydney

WARNER BROS. PRESENTS
A MARK JOHNSON/BALTIMORE PICTURES PRODUCTION AN ALFONSO CUARÓN FILM "A LITTLE PRINCESS"
ELEANOR BRON LIAM CUNNINGHAM AND INTRODUCING LIESEL MATTHEWS MUSIC BY PATRICK DOYLE EXECUTIVE PRODUCERS ALAN C.BLOMQUIST AND AMY EPHRON
SCREENPLAY BY RICHARD LaGRAVENESE AND ELIZABETH CHANDLER BASED ON THE NOVEL BY FRANCES HODGSON BURNETT
G GENERAL AUDIENCES
All Ages Admitted
PRODUCED BY MARK JOHNSON DIRECTED BY ALFONSO CUARÓN

WARNER BROS. FAMILY ENTERTAINMENT

ISBN 0-590-48628-4

12 11 10 9 8 7 6 5 4 3   5 6 7 8 9/9 0/0

Printed in the U.S.A.   40

First Scholastic printing, June 1995

1

India, August 1914

Sara Crewe was not like many other ten-year-old girls. She lived in a mansion in India. Every day she saw elephants, camels, gypsies in long veils, and men wearing turbans. Her father was a captain in the British army. Her mother, an American, had died when Sara was a baby.

Sara knew how to ride an elephant. She could also sing Indian folk songs and speak French. But best of all, Sara made up the most magical stories, stories she sometimes believed were true. For Sara liked nothing better than to dream and think.

One day Sara sat on the banks of the lake with Maya, her Indian nanny. Laki, Maya's son, played in the water with his baby elephant. Maya was telling Sara her favorite story. It was a very old Indian tale about a beautiful princess. . . .

* * *

A long time ago, when the sun sat higher than it does now, there lived a beautiful princess in a land known as India. She was married to the handsome Prince Rama.

The princess lived with her husband in the enchanted forest because Prince Rama's jealous stepmother would not let them live in the kingdom. The princess did not mind. She loved her prince so much, she would have lived with him anywhere.

One day, Princess Sita saw a wounded gazelle in the woods. She begged Rama to go and help it.

The prince was afraid to leave Sita alone. For at the other end of the forest lived the evil ten-headed monster — Ravanna. Rama drew a circle in the ground.

"This is a magic circle," he told Sita. "So long as you stay inside it no harm can come to you."

Sita kissed her prince good-bye and promised she would stay inside the magic circle.

That night, the princess heard a horrible cry. Thinking her beloved Rama was in danger, the princess ran from her circle.

"Rama, Rama!" she called.

The princess soon came upon an old beggar man. He looked so helpless, the kindhearted princess wanted to help him. She had no food or money so she gave him the long beaded bracelet off her wrist.

As soon as he had the bracelet, the beggar became the ten-headed monster — Ravanna! He grabbed the princess and took her to his palace. He wanted to make her his bride.

Far away, Rama bent over the wounded gazelle. His hands moved over the gazelle's body, healing it. A monkey named Hanuman watched Rama from a tree.

As soon as the gazelle was well, Rama rushed off to rejoin his beloved princess. Imagine his horror when he found the magic circle empty.

Princess Sita was now a prisoner in Ravanna's tower. She spent the hours staring out her small window.

One day a bird perched on her windowsill. The princess petted the bird and whispered to it. It seemed to listen to her.

Rama was staring sadly at the empty circle when the bird flew up to him. It sang in his ear telling him what had become of his princess. It led him toward Ravanna's palace.

When Ravanna saw the bird — and the prince — coming toward the tower, he fetched his bow and arrow. His arrow hit the bird, who fell like a stone.

Ravanna then put ten more arrows into his bow. He sent them all high into the air. The smoke from the arrows surrounded Prince Rama.

Although the prince did not know it, Hanuman, the monkey, still followed him. The monkey took a deep breath. He blew the clouds of smoke away from the prince. When the smoke cleared, the monkey saw Rama was dead.

Suddenly, something wonderful happened. The gazelle Rama had healed wandered into the clearing. He curled up next to the fallen prince and brought him back to life.

At once Rama set out to rescue his bride. This time the monkey led the way. As they neared the palace, a giant shadow fell over Rama. It was the shadow of the ten-headed monster. All his ten heads were enormous — and very angry. How dare the prince come to his palace! Ravanna came toward the prince ready to kill him.

Sita watched from her window. She knew the prince was about to die. So she took the locket from around her neck, kissed it, and let it fall out the window.

As the locket reached the ground, it opened. A strange shape rose out of it. The shape rose high in the sky.

Suddenly, the sky darkened with clouds. Thunder rumbled overhead. A bolt of lightning struck Ravanna and killed him.

Sita leaned out her tower window smiling at the prince, as the sun came out over the clouds, and shone all around them.

Sara Crewe had heard that story over and over again. But she never tired of it.

"Did you ever know a real prince?" Sara asked Maya as she petted the baby elephant's trunk.

"Yes . . . Laki's father," her nanny answered.

"I mean real princes and princesss," Sara asked.

"All women are princesses," Maya said. "It is our right."

Sara smiled. Maybe she could be as much of a princess as the beautiful Princess Sita.

2

Sara rode home from the lake on the baby elephant. Laki led Sara and the elephant toward the back of Sara's mansion.

Sara and Laki looked at all the well-dressed men and women strolling outside. Indian servants brought them cool drinks on sparkling silver trays.

The men and women looked at Sara and Laki, too. They were not happy with what they saw. Sara was soaking wet from her swim in the lake, and she wore only her slip.

A group of British children crowded around Sara when the elephant stopped to drink from a fountain. As Laki helped Sara off the elephant, she smiled at him.

"Get that smelly animal out of here," said a bossy twelve-year-old girl named Clara Pideson.

"I will not," Sara answered. "He's thirsty." Sara did not like Clara at all.

"I wasn't talking about the elephant," Clara said in a haughty voice.

Laki bowed his head in shame. Clara and some other children laughed, but not Sara. She was very angry. She marched over to Clara and waved her hands over Clara's head. At the same time, she chanted words that made no sense.

"Stop that! What are you doing?" Clara demanded.

Sara stopped and stared at Clara. "I just put an ancient curse on you," Sara answered calmly. "When you turn twenty, all your hair will fall out. And every time you talk it will be backwards. So your name won't be Clara Pideson, it'll be Aralc Nosedip."

"Aaahhhhh!" Clara screamed.

That evening, Sara stood with her father in a wide meadow. They both watched the sun set over the high Himalayan Mountains.

"I'll miss it here," Sara's father said. "India is the only place on earth that stirs the imagination." He looked down at his daughter and shook his head. "Not that you need any help in *that* department."

Sara grinned. She loved being with her father.

"Aralc Nosedip, huh?" her father asked.

Sara shrugged. "She asked for it."

Captain Andrew Crewe smiled and put his arm around Sara.

"I wish the summer would never end," she said sadly.

Captain Crewe knelt down before his daughter. "It'll be all right, sweetheart. You're going to love America."

"But it's so far away," Sara said. "Why can't I go to school in England? At least we'd be closer to each other."

"England's no place for a young girl until this war is over." Her father's voice was firm. "Besides, you'll be going to the same school your mother went to when she was your age. In a city called New York."

Sara put her head on her father's shoulder. "New York," she said. "What a silly name."

3

On the night before they set sail for America, Sara slept soundly in her pretty room. She woke up when her father kissed her good night.

"Big day tomorrow. Almost like going on an adventure, isn't it?" Captain Crewe asked. He tried to sound cheerful, but Sara could tell he was sad. "I promise we'll spend every minute together until we reach New York."

Sara looked pleased. She smiled even more when she saw a wrapped package on her bed.

Sara sat up to open her present. It was a book of Indian tales. "*The Ramayana*!" Sara exclaimed in delight. *The Ramayana* was a book of very old Indian tales. Sara's favorite story about the princess was in it.

"In there is every story I ever told you," her father said.

"And now I can tell them to myself as if you were

really there. Except I'll never be able to do all those voices as well as you. Especially the monsters."

Captain Crewe wrinkled his nose. "Oh," he said, sounding as if he had a cold. "The monsters have this sort of squeaky, nasal quality."

Sara wrinkled her nose, too. She tried to speak just like her father. "Like this?"

"A bit more wrinkled," her father replied.

" 'Oh cursed prince, thou hast drawn thy last breath,' " Sara said, pretending she had a stuffy nose.

Her father chuckled. "Perfect. You'll do just fine," he said.

"Daddy," Sara said. She sat up a little straighter in her bed. "Maya told me all girls are princesses."

"Maya is a very wise woman," her father answered, smiling. "I believe you are, and always will be, my little princess," he said softly.

The following day, travelers, merchants, servants, and porters crowded on the dock. Captain Crewe made sure the porter loaded their trunks on the big ship. Sara sat on the shore watching the dock scene with wide eyes. It was so hot, she welcomed the cool breeze she suddenly felt on her neck.

Sara turned around to find an Indian man staring at her. A monkey sat on the man's shoulder. Sara stared back at the man, until some people passed in front of him. When the people had walked on, Sara saw the man was gone.

Sara did not know it at the time, but the man's name was Ram Dass. She would see him again in New York.

At that moment the ship's horn blasted. Everyone scrambled aboard. Sara and her father were on their way to America.

That evening, on board the ship, Sara's father gave her a beautiful gold locket. "I gave this to your mother on our wedding day," Captain Crewe explained. "I want you to have it."

Sara looked up at her father. She looked as if she were about to cry. Slowly she opened the locket.

Inside were two pictures. One was of her father. Sara thought he looked just like Prince Rama. The other was of her mother, who looked like the Princess Sita in Sara's dreams.

"She was so beautiful," Sara said proudly. Captain Crewe gently took the locket and fastened it around Sara's neck.

Several weeks later, the ship glided by the Statue of Liberty. Sara and her father were in New York.

4

New York, September 1914

A horse-drawn carriage sped down the bustling city streets. It entered a tree-lined square and stopped in front of a large brownstone house. Captain Crewe helped Sara from the carriage and paid the driver.

Sara slowly walked up the brownstone steps. She read the gold plaque near the front door. It said:

MISS MINCHIN'S SEMINARY FOR GIRLS
Established 1856

Sara took a deep breath before she rang the doorbell. On the second floor of the house, a black servant girl pushed open a window and looked outside. Sara looked up at her.

Amelia Minchin, the sister of the school's principal, opened the front door. Amelia was a plump, cheerful woman. "Hello! You must be Captain

Crewe," she said, eyeing the handsome, well-dressed captain. "Please come in!"

Sara and her father followed Amelia into a large cold hallway. "My sister will be down presently," she told the captain. "We were just preparing the young lady's room. Your beautiful things arrived this morning," she added, looking at Sara.

"Thank you . . ." Captain Crewe answered. He looked a little confused. Amelia had never told him her name.

"Oh! Heavens! Amelia . . . Amelia Minchin," Amelia said as she shook Captain Crewe's hand once again.

Sara smiled. Amelia Minchin seemed all right. Maybe this cold-looking school wouldn't be so bad after all.

As soon as Sara met the other Miss Minchin, she did not feel so happy anymore. The other Miss Minchin was thin and severe. She talked nonstop about school rules. And she never smiled.

"Classes begin promptly at eight o'clock," Miss Minchin told Sara and her father as she led them through the parlor. "We cover all subjects — literature, mathematics, science, and of course French and Latin."

"Oh, Sara speaks fluent — " Captain Crewe began.

Miss Minchin wouldn't let him finish. "Lunch is

served at one-thirty, after which we take our daily walk," she said as she led Sara and her father down a long dreary hallway. "Study hall is from four-thirty to six-thirty, followed by a light supper," she continued.

Sara wondered if Miss Minchin ever stopped talking.

"Before bedtime we read from one of the great classics — something children always look forward to," Miss Minchin added.

Sara frowned. Miss Minchin's Seminary did not sound like too much fun.

Miss Minchin suddenly opened one of the doorways in the hall. Sara and her father followed her into a large classroom. A large group of girls all turned to see the new arrivals. The girls ranged in age from six to twelve. Their French teacher, Monsieur DuFarge, was asleep at his desk.

Miss Minchin coughed loudly. The teacher woke up with a start.

"Girls, I would like you to say hello to our new arrival — Miss Sara Crewe."

"Hello, Sara," the girls said slowly.

"You must tell them about your exciting life in India," Miss Minchin said to Sara in a loud whisper. Then she turned to Sara's father. "No doubt she'll be our most popular student in no time," she added.

Sara looked very embarrassed. All the girls had

heard. One of them, Lavinia, gave Sara a dirty look. At age twelve, Lavinia thought she was the most popular girl in the school. She did not want anyone taking her place, especially not a ten-year-old.

Miss Minchin turned her back on the school girls and led Sara and her father to the window. She needed to tell them the important school rules. Number one — the Communication Rule. To learn concentration, the girls were not allowed to talk, look at, or write one another except during their free time.

Out of the corner of her eye, Sara saw Lavinia reach out and grab the pigtail of a plump girl in front of her. Lavinia dipped the pigtail into her inkwell.

"The Order Rule," Miss Minchin continued, "teaches the girls to attend to their rooms. The Tidiness Rule helps them in caring for their personal appearance."

Sara sighed.

"Also I'm afraid jewelry and other such finery are not allowed." Miss Minchin's voice was firm. She looked pointedly at Sara's locket.

Sara's hand flew to her neck. "Well, could I wear it in my room, during my free time?" she asked politely.

The other students gasped. No one dared argue with Miss Minchin.

"Well, if you absolutely insist," Miss Minchin

said icily. She looked at Sara's father for help.

"I do," Sara said. Captain Crewe grinned at his daughter. It was clear whose side he was on.

Miss Minchin looked very angry. She forced a smile for Captain Crewe's sake. But from that moment on, Miss Minchin took a dislike to her new pupil.

5

Miss Minchin coughed softly. She had now finished showing Sara and her father the school grounds. They stood before her in the school's small courtyard.

"Now I come to the part I find most delicate," she said. " . . . payment."

"Oh, yes," Captain Crewe answered. "My solicitor, Mr. Barrow, has instructions to send payments to you every month." He handed Miss Minchin the lawyer's business card. "Whatever Sara needs, you just let Mr. Barrow know."

Miss Minchin looked very pleased. She proudly led the way up to Sara's room.

Sara had the prettiest room in the school. Her father had made sure of that. The room had corner windows and a large fireplace. Sara's toys and books had arrived. So had her fine clothes. Her father always made sure Sara had the best of everything.

Miss Minchin left Sara and her father alone so they could say their good-byes. They did not have much more time together.

Captain Crewe sat in a chair and pulled his daughter on his lap. "We'll write each other every day," he said as he hugged her.

Sara tried to smile.

"You know," Captain Crewe began. His eyes twinkled. "I think I saw something . . . on that chair over there."

Sara looked up to see a doll's foot behind a chair. She slowly crossed the room and picked up the beautiful new doll.

"She came all the way from France to be with you," Captain Crewe said proudly. "Her name is Emily."

Sara nodded sadly. Her father saw at once the new doll could never take his place. He walked over and knelt beside his daughter.

"You know," Captain Crewe said, "dolls make the very best friends. Just because they can't speak, it doesn't mean they don't listen. Did you know, when we leave them alone, they come to life?"

Sara looked up and shook her head. Her blue eyes brightened.

"Yes," her father said. "Before we walk in and catch them, they return to their places, quick as lightning."

17

"Why don't they come to life in front of us so we can see?" she asked.

"Because it's magic," her father answered. "Magic has to be believed. That's the only way it's real."

Sara looked at her new doll proudly. Her father reached out and stroked his daughter's hair.

"Whenever you miss me terribly," he began, "just tell Emily. She'll get the message to me wherever I am." His voice shook. "And then I'll send one back right away, so that when you hug her, you'll really be getting a hug from me."

Sara was comforted by this thought, but her father looked heartbroken. He bowed his head so Sara wouldn't see the tears in his eyes.

Sara had never seen her father act like this before. She gently took his hand. "It's all right, Papa. I'm going to be fine."

Captain Crewe looked at Sara proudly. "I know," he said softly.

At twilight, Captain Crewe walked to his carriage. He turned to look up at Sara. She waved from her bedroom window.

"Good-bye princess," he called softly.

Sara held Emily tightly. Together they watched her father's carriage pull away from the curb.

6

The following morning the schoolgirls at Miss Minchin's Seminary sat at the large breakfast table. They were all talking about Sara.

"Did you see all her toys?" asked six-year-old Ruth.

"Her father grows crackers or something. They're very rich," said an eight-year-old named Jane.

"Her father is British. I heard he's best friends with the king and queen," added Betsy, who was ten.

Lavinia was growing more and more angry. Why was everyone talking about the new girl? "Hah!" she said loudly, "I heard he was thrown out of India because people died eating his poisoned crackers."

"Really?" answered Gertrude. "I once had an aunt who died from eating poisoned string beans."

"Oh, who cares about her," Lavinia said rudely.

Sara rushed out of her bedroom, still tying her hair ribbon. She knew she was late for breakfast. She closed her door, then stopped. Maybe she could catch Emily moving. She peeked through the keyhole.

Emily was sitting quietly in her chair, just the way Sara had left her. "Boy, she's fast," Sara murmured.

Sara rushed down the stairs. Photographs of past graduating classes hung by the banister. Sara stopped and looked. She searched all the faces until she found her mother's.

"Sara!" Miss Minchin called. She stood at the bottom of the stairs. "We are not accustomed to delaying breakfast for one student."

"I'm sorry, Miss Minchin," Sara said as she went down the stairs. "But I found —"

"You're not the only child here, Sara. You must remember that." Miss Minchin's voice was cold.

Soon after breakfast, Sara went to her math class. She sat in the back of the room.

"Seven times six is forty-two," said Betsy.

"Seven times seven is forty-nine," said Gertrude.

"Seven times eight is fifty-eight. No, no . . . fifty-four. No, wait . . ." said Ermengarde. She turned beet red.

Sara felt sorry for Ermengarde. Ermengarde was the one Lavinia always picked on. Just yesterday Lavinia had dipped Ermengarde's hair in her inkwell.

"I'm sorry, Miss Minchin. I studied for hours last night. Honest, I did," Ermengarde said.

Miss Minchin gave Ermengarde a cold stare. "I find that very hard to believe. I imagine your father will as well."

"Oh, please don't tell him, Miss Minchin." Ermengarde sounded horrified.

"Lavinia, you may continue," Miss Minchin said, ignoring poor Ermengarde.

Lavinia smirked. "Seven times eight is fifty-six."

Later that day, the girls played in the school courtyard in groups. Sara sat alone, reading *The Ramayana*. Ermengarde, also alone, whispered math tables to herself.

Sara looked up from her reading. Lavinia and her sidekick, Jesse, were giggling at her. Sara tried to ignore them.

Suddenly Amelia appeared at the door. "Sara! Miss Minchin would like to see you in your room right away."

Sara looked surprised. Lavinia and Jesse giggled more loudly. They must have something to do with this, Sara thought to herself.

Sara slowly went up to her room. What she saw made her stop and gasp. Her beautiful clothes and toys had been scattered all over the floor.

Miss Minchin stood in the middle of the mess. She was trying on one of Sara's silk capes in front of the mirror. Sara stood watching her, unsure of what to do. "Miss Minchin?" she finally said in a timid voice.

Miss Minchin whirled around. She had not known Sara was watching her. She was ashamed to have been caught trying on her clothes. That made her even angrier. "This room is a disgrace! I want it picked up immediately. Is that clear?" Miss Minchin said. She threw the cape on the chair and stormed out of the room.

7

It was late in the afternoon when Sara finished straightening up her room. She sat in her window seat with Emily writing a letter to her father.

Dear Papa,
   Things are fine, except that everybody here seems to be mad at me . . . in the same way Clara back home was always mad. I don't see how you can go from one end of the world to the other and still meet the same people. . . .

Sara paused. She noticed two men on the street below. The men stood in front of the brownstone next to the school. One was an older man. The other was a young soldier in uniform. As they tearfully hugged one another good-bye, Sara was reminded of saying good-bye to her own father. A teardrop fell on her letter.

Sara did not know how long she had been crying when she suddenly heard loud noises outside her room. Someone was having a tantrum — not a little one either but a full-scale one with lots of shrieking and kicking.

"Lottie, you mustn't get so upset. Here play with your music box," Amelia was saying. Lottie only howled more loudly.

"Oh, you wicked child. I'll shake you, I will." Amelia sounded desperate. "Please stop screaming. How about a cookie? Would you like that?"

Amelia rushed downstairs to the kitchen for a cookie. A second later, Sara opened her bedroom door. She stood for a moment, calmly watching the screaming little girl. "You know," Sara said finally, "it's very hard to study with you carrying on like this."

"I want my mama!" Lottie wailed.

"You'll see her soon," Sara said, above the shrieks.

"No, I won't! She's dead. I won't ever see her again!"

Sara walked over to Lottie. "Well, I don't have a mother either."

Lottie suddenly stopped screaming. She looked interested. "You don't? Where is she?"

"In heaven," Sara answered simply. "But that

doesn't mean I can't talk to her. I tell her everything and I know she hears me."

"How?" Lottie asked. She'd stopped kicking and screaming by now.

"Because that's what angels do."

"Your mama's an angel?" Lottie sounded delighted by this.

Sara knelt beside the little girl. "Of course. And so is yours," Sara answered. "With wings of silk and a crown of golden roses." Lottie's eyes grew wider as Sara kept talking, making up a wonderful story as she went along.

Sara told Lottie their mothers lived together in a castle surrounded by hundreds of flowers — and filled with music.

Down the hall, Ermengarde opened her door a little so she could hear Sara's story. The servant girl, Becky, peeked over the top stair. She didn't want to miss a word.

Just then Becky's shoe squeaked on the stair. Sara turned in time to see Becky jump up and rush toward the attic door like a frightened mouse.

"Oh, wait," Sara called after her. But Becky had disappeared up the attic staircase.

"That's Becky," Lottie tried to explain to Sara. "We're not allowed to talk to her."

"Why not?" Sara wondered.

"She's a servant girl — and she has dark skin."

"*So?*" Sara asked sharply.

"Well, doesn't that mean something?" Lottie asked. She looked rather confused.

Sara was curious about Becky. So, later that afternoon, she climbed the narrow attic staircase and pushed open the door to Becky's room.

Becky sat on her narrow cot in the dark, bare room. She had not heard Sara come in. She was too busy taking off her old shoes that looked much too small for her. Sara was shocked to see how swollen and blistered Becky's feet were.

Suddenly a board creaked under Sara's feet. Becky whirled around and jumped to her feet.

"Oh, I'm sorry. I didn't mean . . ." Sara stammered. For once she couldn't think of anything to say.

"Is there anything I can do for you, miss? I just came up to change my shoes."

"No, nothing," Sara replied.

"Well then. Begging your pardon, but we'll both be in trouble if you stay," Becky said. She watched Sara guardedly. Sara nodded and left the room.

The following day, Becky found a wrapped box and a note on her cot. She opened the note and read:

Dear Becky,

I'm sorry. Hope we can still be friends.

Sara

Inside the box was a pair of furry slippers. Becky gratefully slid them on her tired feet.

8

In the evenings, the girls of Miss Minchin's Seminary gathered in the parlor for their nightly reading. Tonight, they took turns reading from a dull English novel. Miss Minchin and Amelia listened sleepily from their chairs.

Ermengarde read the boring story without expression. The other girls fell asleep or fidgeted in their chairs. How they hated these evenings. Only Sara appeared to be listening to the story. The plot made her angry. How could the heroine in the book marry a man against her will?

When it was her turn to read, Sara decided to change the ending. She had Charlotte, the heroine, run away from home with her lover Pierre. The two set sail for a tropical island and were captured by a band of pirates!

When they heard Sara's new ending, the girls began to stir in their chairs. They nudged one another awake and listened to every word.

Miss Minchin began to sense something was wrong. She grabbed the book from Sara and thumbed through it. Sara calmly continued. "Charlotte and Pierre threw themselves overboard — and were rescued by a band of mermaids."

The girls gasped in delight. Miss Minchin threw the book down.

"Stop!" she cried to Sara. "What do you think you're doing?"

"I imagined a different ending," Sara explained.

"You imagined it," Miss Minchin said scornfully.

Sara nodded. "Don't you ever do that Miss Minchin? Believe in something just to make it seem real?"

"I suppose that's rather easy for a child who has everything," Miss Minchin replied.

Sara looked hurt.

"From now on, there will be no more 'make-believe' during reading hour or at any other time in this school. Is that understood?" Miss Minchin's voice was firm.

The girls slowly climbed the stairs to the bedrooms. They were sorry not to have heard the end of Sara's story. Sara, Ermengarde, Betsy, and Gertrude were the last to head up the stairs.

"I've never heard a story like that in my whole life!" Betsy exclaimed.

"You must know a lot more good stories like that," Ermengarde said proudly.

"I have an idea," Betsy said to Sara. Her eyes twinkled. "After Minchin goes to bed, we'll sneak into your room, and you can show us what a real story is."

"Oh, yes, yes!" Ermengarde and Betsy said at once.

"Well," Sara answered. "Maybe if it's just you three."

That night, many more than three girls crowded into Sara's room to hear the story of Princess Sita. Each night Sara told them a new chapter.

Before long, Sara could write her father with good news. She had some friends — Ermengarde, Lottie, Betsy, and Gertrude. Best of all, she had a secret friend, Becky. In a way, Sara felt closer to Becky than she did to any of the other girls. Though she missed her father terribly, she was beginning to like Miss Minchin's Seminary a little better.

9

Far away, on an English battlefield, Captain Crewe read his daughter's latest letter with tears in his eyes. He wished he could be with her.

"Captain!" a soldier interrupted Crewe's daydream. "Colonel Harding just called. The enemy line is advancing. Our orders are to retreat immediately."

Captain Crewe looked around him. What few troops the army had left looked scared and numb. "Start moving out," he said.

Captain Crewe picked up his gear and began to follow his troops. Suddenly he heard someone groaning at his feet. He knelt beside the young soldier who lay wounded on the ground. The young man shook with a fever.

"Hey, we need a medic here!" Captain Crewe shouted. But the others had already gone off. Captain Crewe took off his jacket and wrapped it around the young soldier. Then he lifted him over his shoulder and walked as quickly as he could. He could hear German war planes overhead.

As the sound of the planes grew closer, Captain Crewe froze. He quickly lowered the soldier and pulled the two of them against the trench wall.

The war planes dropped poison gas on the deserted battlefield. Soon clouds of yellow smoke moved toward Captain Crewe and the young soldier. Captain Crewe began to choke. He tied a handkerchief around the young soldier's face. Then he climbed out of the trench and tried to pull the soldier out with him. But the gas soon overpowered them both.

Slowly, Captain Crewe lost consciousness. The young soldier slid back into the trench. Crewe's body lay still upon the ground.

10

At Miss Minchin's Seminary, the parlor had been decorated for a birthday party. A big cake with twelve candles sat on the table. The girls crowded around Sara as she blew out her candles and began to cut the cake. Miss Minchin and Amelia watched from the door.

"I want a big piece!" Lottie reminded Sara.

"Oh, hush up, Lottie," Lavinia said rudely. "I'm sure *Princess* Sara will give everyone a fair share. Right, princess?" Lavinia added turning to Sara.

Lottie gave Sara a sheepish look. "I told her that's what you were," Lottie explained.

"Not just me," Sara said. "All girls are princesses. Even snotty two-faced bullies like you, Lavinia."

Lavinia glared at Sara, but the other girls giggled. Miss Minchin frowned and was about to scold Sara when the doorbell rang. Before she went to answer the door, Miss Minchin gave Sara a disapproving look.

Mr. Barrow, Captain Crewe's lawyer, stood at the door.

"May I speak with you in private?" he asked Miss Minchin.

"Yes, of course. Right this way," Miss Minchin said as she led the lawyer into her office.

"Before you begin, Mr. Barrow, may I just say that Sara is quite the favorite around here," Miss Minchin said. "We went to great expense to make this a special birthday. I'm afraid your check to us this month will be rather large."

"There will be no more checks, Miss Minchin," the lawyer answered. His face looked somber.

"Excuse me?" Miss Minchin asked. She could not believe her ears.

The lawyer stepped into her office and closed the door.

While Miss Minchin talked to the lawyer, the party grew merrier and merrier. The older girls played a game with Sara. They put a blindfold over her head and had her try to tag them. Amelia and Ermengarde played a jazz tune on the piano. Soon everyone swung their hips and tapped their feet to the music.

Miss Minchin appeared at the doorway and

watched the scene in silence. Suddenly, she stormed over to the piano and slammed the lid on the keys. Amelia and the girls fell silent. They had never seen Miss Minchin look so angry.

Miss Minchin then tore off Sara's blindfold. "This party is over," she announced. "I want everyone to go to their rooms."

"But, we . . ." Sara began.

"Sara," Miss Minchin said in her coldest voice, "you will stay behind. I have something to tell you."

The girls scrambled out the door. They were all frightened by Miss Minchin's tone.

"Amelia, go to Sara's room and find a simple black dress," Miss Minchin ordered.

"But — " Amelia protested.

"Do as I say!" Miss Minchin snapped. As Amelia hurried away, Miss Minchin turned again to Sara.

"Why will I need a black dress?" Sara asked, puzzled.

"I'm afraid I have some bad news, Sara," Miss Minchin began. "Your father has . . ." She paused and took a deep breath. "Your father has died. He was killed in battle several weeks ago."

Sara turned pale. She sat down in the nearest chair and stared out the window, not moving. Miss Minchin continued. "The war left his company without any money. You are now penniless. And you have no relatives who can take care of you."

Sara continued to look out the window. She didn't say a word.

"What are you staring at?" Miss Minchin snapped. She was a little scared of Sara. "Don't you understand what I am saying? You are alone in the world, unless I decide to keep you here!"

Sara and Miss Minchin did not see Becky hiding behind the door. Becky had heard every word. She felt frightened for Sara.

Outside a storm brewed. Thunder rumbled overhead.

"Your clothes, your toys, everything now belongs to me. Though they will hardly make up for the money I spent on your party," Miss Minchin continued. Rain pelted the windowpane. Sara did not look up.

Miss Minchin cleared her throat. "From now on, you must earn your room and board here." Sara was making her more and more nervous. Why didn't the child say anything?

"You will be moved to the attic with Becky and work as a servant — cleaning, running errands, and helping Mabel in the kitchen," Miss Minchin finished.

11

That evening, Miss Minchin led Sara to her attic room in the tower. The light from Miss Minchin's candles flickered on the dirty walls.

Sarah now wore a simple black dress. She clutched Emily and her bedding. She slowly followed Miss Minchin up the narrow staircase.

"If you don't do as you are told, you'll be thrown out," Miss Minchin reminded Sara. Sara's eyes widened. She did not want to be alone and homeless in New York City.

Miss Minchin opened the door to Sara's attic room. It was next to Becky's. The walls were made from rotten wooden planks. Cobwebs hung in every corner. The low slanting roof leaked from the skylight.

"You will report to Mabel in the kitchen at five AM," Miss Minchin said. As she turned to go, she saw Sara carried a book and her locket inside a blanket.

Miss Minchin took the locket and glared. "I could have you arrested for taking this," she said. "I expect you to remember, Sara Crewe . . . you're not a princess any longer," she said as she left the room.

Sara sat alone in the dark. Her walls creaked. The wind banged against the shutters of her small window. And rain dripped from the skylight.

Sara trembled. She drew a big circle on the floor with a piece of coal from the fireplace. Then she curled up inside the circle and cried and cried. "Papa . . . Papa," she called.

12

The next morning at breakfast, the girls could not stop whispering. When Sara came out of the kitchen carrying a large bowl of oatmeal, they fell silent.

"Sara, what happened?" Lottie whispered as Sara served her.

"Sara!" Miss Minchin called sharply. She stood at the doorway. "You are to serve the girls without talking!"

Miss Minchin turned toward the girls. "Sara will be working here as a servant," she explained. "You are not to speak to her."

The girls all nodded. Ermengarde stared at her bowl when Sara served her. She did not know what to do.

"Morning, Miss Amelia," said Frances the milk-man as he came in the kitchen. Frances liked Amelia.

"Oh, good morning, Frances," Amelia answered. She fixed her hair with one hand.

Sara held a tray of breakfast dishes and watched them. Frances unpacked the milk bottles and complimented Amelia on how well she looked. Amelia flushed with pleasure.

Mabel the cook watched Sara and saw she wasn't doing anything. "Hurry up and rinse those dishes!" she snapped. Sara rushed to obey her.

Each day for Sara became drearier than the last. She woke early to serve breakfast, wash dishes, mop floors, and do errands. Miss Minchin and Mabel kept after her all the time. They loved having someone to boss around, especially someone who once had everything.

Her hands became red and blistered. Her few dresses began to look worn and frayed. Her shoes had holes in them.

One day while Sara was out doing errands, a gust of wind blew her thin shawl off her shoulders. With a cry, Sara ran after it. The shawl landed in the square by the school — right at a man's feet.

Sara looked up at the man in surprise. He was Indian, and she knew she had seen him before. He was the man who had stared at her on the docks. Again the man stared at Sara as she picked up her shawl.

Suddenly, they both heard a cry. Sara turned to

see. She watched as two soldiers in uniform delivered a telegram to Mr. Randolph, the old man who lived next door to the school.

The Indian man left Sara and went to stand at Mr. Randolph's side. The Indian man must live next door, too, Sara thought to herself.

Mr. Randolph read the telegram, then collapsed against the Indian man and wept. "Not my son," he moaned. "Please, not John."

Sara remembered seeing Mr. Randolph say goodbye to his son. It seemed so long ago, now. The young man must have been killed, just like her father.

"Sara!" Miss Minchin called from the doorway. Sara jumped and hurried back to school.

That evening, Sara sat on a crate in her room, looking out the window. Suddenly a wooden plank in the wall creaked even more loudly than usual. Sara turned in time to see Becky squeeze through a small opening in the wall.

"Sara," Becky asked gently. "Why don't you tell your stories anymore?"

"Stories . . ." Sara said softly.

"They might make you feel better," Becky urged her friend.

Sara shook her head. "They're just make-believe. They don't mean anything."

"They've always meant something to me," Becky

insisted. "There were days I thought I'd die till I heard you talk about the magic."

Sara stared out the window. "There is no magic, Becky."

Becky looked heartbroken to see Sara like this. She turned and silently went back to her room.

Sara sat alone in the dark and whispered, "Papa, can you hear me? I'm so scared." She picked Emily up off the floor. "Can he hear me, Emily?"

Emily remained still. "Oh, you're nothing but a doll!" Sara cried as she tossed Emily back on the floor.

Becky lay awake for a long time on the other side of Sara's wall. She could hear Sara crying well into the night.

13

The girls at Miss Minchin's school paired up in the school courtyard for their daily walk. Sara raked leaves in the corner. Timidly, Lottie broke away from her companions and approached Sara.

"Sara, are you still a princess?" she asked her friend.

It was the first time any of the girls had spoken to Sara since her birthday party. She turned in surprise.

"Get back in line, Lottie," she said softly. "We'll both be in trouble." She did not tell Lottie she no longer believed in princesses.

"Lottie!" Miss Minchin called as she stepped outside ready to take the girls on the walk. Lottie hurried back to her place in line. Ermengarde glanced back at Sara, and Sara looked up at her and smiled. Because Miss Minchin was there, Ermengarde was too afraid to smile back.

Sara felt hurt. She went back to her raking, while Ermengarde lowered her head in shame and followed the group out.

One cold winter evening, Sara wandered through New York's busy meat market. The smell of all the food made her feel faint from hunger. Sara had had no supper. Quickly, she bought the supplies Mabel needed and hurried back to school.

On the way home, she began to feel so tired. The packages felt like lead in her arms. She put them down and leaned against a shop window to rest. A well-dressed boy walked down the street with his mother.

The boy looked at Sara. He pressed a coin into her hand. "Here, little girl," he said.

Sara looked up in shock. Slowly, she turned to see her reflection in the shop window. No wonder the boy had given her money. Her clothes looked like rags. Her face was pale and pinched. She looked just like one of New York's many street beggars.

Sara stared some more. She was looking into the window of a bakery. Cakes, pies, fresh bread, and buns filled the shop window. Sara walked inside.

Soon, Sara sat on the stoop outside the bakery. She fished the hot steaming bun out of its bag and held it to her mouth. Suddenly she saw something that stopped her from eating.

A tired beggar woman walked down the street holding a baby and a basket of yellow roses. Sara watched as the woman tried in vain to sell the roses. No one would buy any from her.

Sara slowly walked over to the woman and handed her hot bun to the baby. The woman looked at Sara in surprise. She did not expect such kindness from someone who looked as poor as she did.

"Wait!" she called as Sara turned away. Quickly she handed her a yellow rose from her basket. "For the princess," she said, smiling.

Sara smiled back. She was too moved to answer. Swiftly, she picked up her packages and hurried back to Miss Minchin's. As she passed Mr. Randolph's house, she saw a black bow on his front door. The old man sat by the fireplace, his head bowed. Sara put her yellow rose on his doorstep.

That evening, the moonlight flooded into Sara's attic room. Sara lay on her cot, staring at a mouse. The mouse stared back at Sara, twitching his whiskers.

"What is it, little mouse? Are you a prisoner, too?" Sara asked him.

It was so cold in the room, Sara could see her breath. She shivered under her thin blanket.

On the other side of the wall, Becky shivered, too. She paused, then knocked on the wall. "Sara, are you awake?" she called.

"Yes," Sara answered.

"Is it ever this cold where you come from?" Becky wanted to know.

"No," Sara answered softly.

"Tell me, Sara. Tell me again about India," Becky pleaded.

Sara sighed. "Well, the air is so hot there, you can almost taste it."

Becky smiled. It was the first time Sara had told her a story since her father died. "I bet it tastes like coconuts," she answered.

"No," Sara said, thinking. "The air smells more like spices — curry and saffron. . . ."

Sara drifted off to sleep, dreaming about India. When she woke up, moonlight still poured through her window. She saw her bed was covered with snow. Outside, she heard a man's voice singing an Indian folksong — the folksong she used to sing in India.

Sara climbed out of bed and looked out. In a window across the way was a man in a turban — the same man who always stared at Sara when he saw her. Slowly the man bowed to her. Sara couldn't take her eyes off him. Then just as slowly, she bowed to him. It was as if a spell had been broken.

Sara lifted her arms and began to dance around her room. She felt strangely at peace. For the first time since her father died, she felt like a princess.

14

The following morning, Sara saw the Indian man outside. A monkey perched on his shoulder.

"Hanuman," Sara said, greeting them. Hanuman was the name of the monkey in *The Ramayana*.

The Indian man smiled to hear Sara knew something about India. He greeted her in his native language. This time Sara grinned. She understood him perfectly.

Just then, the school's back door opened. Miss Minchin stood in the doorway with the school's chimney sweep.

"You can forget being paid this week," Miss Minchin told the sweep angrily. "I told you I don't want the slightest bit of dirt in this house. Just look at my boot, it's filthy."

"But . . ." the poor sweep protested. He looked thin and tired, and he was covered with dirt.

"Out, out!" Miss Minchin cried.

The sweep trudged down the street. Before he left, he deposited his big bags of soot by the garbage bin near Sara.

Sara looked at the bags of soot. They gave her an idea.

Later that day, Sara carried a bag of soot to her room. Leaning out her window, she carefully handed the bag to Becky, who was on the roof.

Soon Sara joined Becky on the roof. Together, they tipped the bag toward the chimney. A few specks of ash trickled down to the fireplace in Miss Minchin's study.

Miss Minchin sat at her desk correcting papers. When she heard pieces of ash falling through the chimney, she stopped her work and bent down to look in the fireplace.

Whoosh!! The whole load of ash ran down the chimney. It covered Miss Minchin in black soot. "Aahhh!!" she screamed.

That evening, at dinner, everyone noticed Miss Minchin looked a little strange. She had scrubbed and scrubbed her face with soap and water. Even so, it still looked gray from all the soot, except for two circles around the eyes where her glasses had been.

The school girls could not stop laughing when

they saw her. Ermengarde watched Sara and Becky exchange smiles. Somehow, she knew they were behind all this. She felt left out.

Later that evening Ermengarde climbed the attic stairs. She pushed open Sara's door.

"Is there where you live?" she asked in a choked voice.

Sara looked at her friend in surprise. "You shouldn't be here Ermengarde," was all she said.

Ermengarde felt tears in her eyes. "Oh, Sara, why don't you like me anymore? Did I do something wrong?"

Sara looked stunned. "No, of course not. I just didn't think you wanted me as a friend, now that . . . now that things are different."

"Oh, Sara, no," Ermengarde protested. "I couldn't get along without you."

Sara looked touched. "I'm sorry Ermengarde. I should've known you wouldn't be like the others." The girls smiled at one another.

Suddenly, they both heard a knock on the wall. Ermengarde jumped. "What's that?" she asked.

Sara moved over to the wall. "One knock means I'm here," she explained to Ermengarde as she knocked on the wall. "Two knocks means all is well. Three knocks means the demon Minchinweed is asleep."

"Oh, Sara, it all sounds so adventurous," Ermengarde said after Becky came through the wall. "I've missed your stories so much. Won't you tell me what happened to Rama and the princess?"

Sara nodded and smiled.

15

One morning in the very early spring, Hanuman the monkey decided to go for a walk. He walked across the wooden plank that connected his master's window with Sara's.

Sara was lacing her shoe when the monkey pushed her shutter open. "Hanuman!" she cried, surprised. "What are you doing here?"

Hanuman climbed on her shoulder and put his hands over her eyes. Sara giggled.

That day, Miss Minchin led the girls on their daily walk. As they strolled down Fifth Avenue, Ermengarde told Betsy and Gertrude all about visiting Sara in the attic. "I can't go every evening because Minchin might find out," Ermengarde explained. "I wait for Sara's signal. Then I know it's safe."

"Oh, how exciting!" Gertrude exclaimed.

"Does Sara understand about us not speaking to her?" Betsy asked.

"Oh, yes," Ermengarde answered. "She pretends Minchin put a spell on all of you to be silent. But I broke the spell because of my courage," she added proudly.

Betsy sighed. "We should make it up to her," she said as she looked at Miss Minchin. "Think," she told her friends. "What's the worst thing Minchin ever did to her?"

"She took her locket away," Ermengarde suggested. "That's it," she said. Her eyes glowed. Ermengarde had a plan.

The next day, Betsy tiptoed to Miss Minchin's office door and peeked through the keyhole. She was waiting for Miss Minchin to leave. Finally, she saw the headmistress put on her coat. Amelia sat at her sister's desk correcting Latin papers.

As Miss Minchin opened her office door to leave, Betsy smiled at her innocently. Miss Minchin gave her a strange look and headed down the hall.

Ermengarde was stationed by the front door. She also smiled. "Good-bye, Miss Minchin," she said sweetly. Miss Minchin nodded. She looked a little suspicious.

Ermengarde waited until she saw the headmistress walking down the sidewalk. Then she signaled to Betsy. Again Betsy looked through the keyhole. Amelia sat back in Miss Minchin's chair. She put her feet on Miss Minchin's desk.

Betsy nodded to Gertrude who was at the bottom of the stairs. Gertrude looked upstairs and nodded to Lottie. At Gertrude's signal, Lottie took a deep breath and began one of her famous tantrums. "Waahhh!!!" she wailed.

Becky came out of the kitchen just in time to see Amelia rush upstairs to Lottie. Becky watched as Ermengarde, Betsy, and Gertrude slipped into Miss Minchin's office. The three girls shut the door.

"The locket has to be in here somewhere," Betsy insisted as she began searching Miss Minchin's desk.

Lottie continued to wail and shriek. Becky stood near Miss Minchin's office door, not knowing what to do. She did not know what was happening.

Outside, Miss Minchin discovered she had left one of her gloves on her desk. Quickly she headed back to school. The headmistress could hear Lottie's tantrum even before she opened the front door. She shook her head in disgust.

"Will you please get that child under control," she snapped at Amelia. Then she stormed toward her office. Becky watched in horror as Miss Minchin stepped to her office door and turned the doorknob.

Inside the office, Ermengarde found the locket

in a drawer. She held it up excitedly. Just then, the door opened. The three girls inside froze.

Becky thought quickly. Before Miss Minchin could enter her office, she screamed — very loudly. Miss Minchin jumped back from her door and glared at Becky.

"Well, what is it?" she said coldly.

"I . . . I . . ." Becky struggled to find an excuse. The three girls smiled at her gratefully as they tip-toed out behind Miss Minchin's back. Miss Minchin never noticed them. Her eyes were still on Becky.

"I thought I saw a mouse," Becky said finally. Miss Minchin sniffed disdainfully and turned back to her office. She ran right into her closed door.

16

Spring came slowly in New York. But it did come. The same day Ermengarde found Sara's locket, Sara found a nest of baby birds under the school's front window.

She started to lean toward the nest when she heard some noise next door. Sara turned in time to see Ram Dass load Mr. Randolph's wheelchair into the waiting carriage. He then climbed in next to his master.

"The young man they found may not be John," Sara heard Ram Dass say.

"Of course he is," Mr. Randolph answered. He then asked the driver to go to St. Mary's Hospital. Sara watched the carriage drive away down the street.

"Sara, didn't I tell you to go to the market?" Mabel said as she appeared on the front step.

"Yes, ma'am," Sara said, rushing off.

* * *

At St. Mary's Hospital, Doctor Reed stood next to Mr. Randolph. They both stared at a man asleep in a hospital bed. Layers of bandages covered the man's eyes. Ram Dass stood in the doorway watching his master.

"He's suffering from acute amnesia, one of the rare side effects of poison gas," the doctor told Mr. Randolph. "His eyes will heal in time. His memory, who can say?"

Mr. Randolph stared sadly at the patient. "He's not my son," he said quietly.

The doctor looked discouraged. "I'm sorry, Mr. Randolph. He was found in severe shock with no coat, no identification. We thought he might be John."

Ram Dass walked toward his master and put his hand on his shoulder. "I'm sorry, sahib."

Mr. Randolph sadly wheeled his chair away.

Outside the hospital, Mr. Randolph turned toward Ram Dass. "You must think me a fool," he told his servant. "A wise man would not have come."

"That soldier needs to be cared for," Ram Dass said.

"He's not my responsibility," Mr. Randolph answered.

"This soldier was in John's regiment. If his memory returns, he might tell sahib what happened to his son," Ram Dass reminded his master.

Mr. Randolph began to look interested. Together, they made plans to bring the wounded soldier home.

17

That evening, Ermengarde, Betsy, Lottie, and Gertrude poked their heads out of their rooms. They waited until Miss Minchin turned out all the lights and closed her bedroom door. Then they tiptoed, in their nightgowns, to the attic door.

Becky sat on Sara's bed holding her hands in front of Sara's eyes. "What's happening?" Sara asked Becky as she heard footsteps on the attic stairs.

"It's a surprise," Becky whispered excitedly.

Just then the door opened. Ermengarde led Betsy, Gertrude, and Lottie into the room. Becky took her hands away so Sara could see.

"What are you doing here?" Sara asked.

"We brought you something," Ermengarde said. She looked at the others. Betsy, Gertrude, and Lottie had never been in Sara's room before. They looked around in shock. Ermengarde coughed to get their attention.

The five girls lined up in front of Sara. "Princess Sara, we would like to present you with something we rescued," Ermengarde began.

"In a most daring adventure," Betsy added. Lottie stepped forward and handed the gold locket to Sara.

For a few moments Sara could think of nothing to say. Tears came to her eyes. "You are all the best friends anyone could ever ask for," she said finally as she hugged them.

Suddenly, the girls heard a loud screech at the window. Hanuman the monkey was perched on the sill outside Sara's window. Everyone except Sara and Becky screamed and dove under the bed.

"It's all right," Sara assured them. She introduced them to Hanuman.

"W-where did he come from?" Lottie asked.

"Right next door — look," Becky said. She pointed to the wooden plank that connected Sara's window to Ram Dass's.

"He comes to visit me all the time, don't you?" Sara asked the monkey.

"Can you really talk to him, Sara?" Betsy asked.

"Yes. Hanuman, say hello to my friends," Sara said. Hanuman turned to the girls, bowed his head, and squealed. Everyone giggled.

Hanuman perched on Sara's shoulder while she told the girls a story. They had insisted she continue telling them of Princess Sita and Prince Rama.

When Sara arrived at the part about Ravanna, the ten-headed monster, the monkey leaped off her shoulder. He landed on Ermengarde's head. The girls all screamed in fright.

Miss Minchin poked her head out of her bedroom door. She thought she heard a noise upstairs.

The girls had all heard Miss Minchin's door creak open. No one dared say a word until they heard the door close.

"Maybe we'd better save the rest of the story for later," Sara suggested. She picked up Hanuman and went to the window. The girls gathered around to say good-bye to him.

At that moment, Miss Minchin entered Sara's attic room. *"What is going on here?!"* she asked sharply.

The girls spun around and cowered. Miss Minchin had rarely looked angrier. Sara quickly hid the locket in the palm of her hand. "It's not their fault," she said. "I . . . I asked them to come."

Miss Minchin clenched her jaw. She turned to her students first. "You four get downstairs immediately," she said in her iciest tone. Ermengarde, Betsy, Gertrude, and Lottie did not have to be told twice. Quickly, they scampered out the door.

"Becky, you will remain locked in your room for the entire day tomorrow without meals," Miss Minchin continued. *"Go!"*

After Becky hurried away, Miss Minchin turned to Sara. "And you," she added, "will perform all her chores in addition to your own. You will go without breakfast, lunch, and dinner."

Sara stared at Miss Minchin and did not say anything. That only made the headmistress angrier.

"Sara Crewe, it is time you learned that real life has nothing to do with your little fantasy games," Miss Minchin said. "Do you understand me?"

"Yes, ma'am," Sara answered. Miss Minchin turned to go.

"But I don't believe in it," Sara added.

Miss Minchin slowly turned and faced Sara again. "Don't tell me you still fancy yourself a princess," she said with a sneer. "Look in a mirror, child."

Sara continued to stare steadily at Miss Minchin. "I am a princess," she said firmly. "All girls are. Even if they live in tiny old attics. Even if they dress in rags. Even if they aren't beautiful or young or smart. They're still princesses." Sara paused. "Didn't your father ever tell you that?" she asked.

Miss Minchin stared at her, speechless. No, no one had ever loved her, or told her they loved her. But she did not say that to Sara. Instead, she only became angrier.

"If I find you up here with any of the other girls again, I'll throw you out into the street," she warned. Then she stormed out of the room.

18

After Miss Minchin left, Sara sat on her cot and opened her locket. She smiled sadly at her mother's picture. Becky came through the opening in the wall and sat next to her.

"What are we going to do?" Becky said sadly. "A whole day with nothing to eat." Becky's stomach rumbled. She was so hungry, she began to cry.

Sara put her arms around her friend.

"I'm scared," Becky told her. "If Minchin throws me out, I've got no place to go. No family . . . nobody wanting me."

"That's not true," Sara answered. "I'm here with you. I've always thought of us as sisters."

"You have?" Becky sounded surprised.

"Of course," Sara answered. "Why don't we make a promise right now to always look out for each other. No matter what happens, we'll never be alone."

"It's a promise," Becky said as she hugged Sara.

"Now," said Sara. "What are we going to do about food?"

"Starve, I guess," Becky answered.

"No," Sara said, shaking her head. "We'll eat a great feast before we go to sleep."

"Feast?" Becky asked, looking around the small room. "What feast?"

"Don't you see that table over there?" Sara said. She motioned toward her rickety crate. "It's covered with a beautiful cloth and candles. And trays and trays of good things to eat."

"But, I don't see any food," Becky insisted.

"Try, Becky. Just make believe," Sara almost pleaded.

Becky looked at the crate and thought for a moment. "Muffins," she finally said.

"Good!" Sara said. "What kind?"

"Every kind of muffin God ever made. And all of them hot!"

Sara looked pleased. "Mmm, smell those sausages," she said as she pretended to lift a lid off a tray.

"Oh, I love sausages," Becky said.

Sara and Becky talked well into the night about what they would eat, and what they would wear to their elegant banquet.

Across the way, Ram Dass petted Hanuman and

watched the girls from his window. He could hear their conversation, and it touched him. It also gave him an idea.

The following morning Hanuman tried very hard to wake Sara by tickling her face. Sara stirred sleepily. She felt a thick, silk quilt over her and the warm glow of a real fire in her fireplace. She closed her eyes smiling. What a wonderful dream this was.

Hanuman squealed and ran away. This time Sara woke up. She looked around her, stunned.

Her room had been transformed. A fire crackled merrily in the grate. A plush rug covered the floor. Silk fabric draped the walls and flowers filled the room. A pretty tablecloth covered the old crate, and on it sat trays of food and two place settings.

Sara looked down at her bed. Becky was still asleep next to her. A thick down quilt covered them. At the foot of the bed were two pairs of slippers and two beautiful robes.

Becky soon woke up and gasped when she saw the room. "I think maybe you went a little too far this time," Becky said. She sounded scared.

"It wasn't me," Sara answered.

Becky and Sara slipped on their new robes and slippers. "I feel like I've been touched by an angel," Becky said.

Sara lifted the lid off a tray of sausages. "Look, just what we ordered," she said.

"I'm a little scared about all this," Becky said.

"Me too," Sara said nodding. "Do you think we shouldn't eat it?"

"I'm not that scared," Becky said. The girls laughed and helped themselves to the delicious food.

19

That morning, the wounded soldier from the hospital ate breakfast in Ram Dass's room. His china matched the china set Sara and Becky were using next door. His eyes were still covered in bandages.

"I will help you," Ram Dass told the soldier as he placed a warm muffin in his hand.

"Thank you for all your kindness," the soldier said.

"It is nothing, sahib," Ram Dass answered.

The soldier sat up at the sound of the word *sahib*. "That word," he said. "It sounds so familiar, and yet, I don't know what it means."

"It is not English," Ram Dass said. "We use it where I am from — in India."

"India," the soldier said softly.

"You know it?" Ram Dass asked.

The soldier tried to remember. "No," he finally

answered. "Everything's a blur. Maybe someday, I'll sort it out."

"You will, sahib," Ram Dass said kindly.

That evening, a full moon hung in the sky. Sara leaned out her window. She watched as Amelia tossed a heavy suitcase to the ground. Frances the milkman waited outside to catch it.

To Sara's surprise, Amelia then heaved herself out the window. Soon the two drove off together in Frances's milk wagon. Amelia and Frances had eloped.

Sara was not surprised. She knew Amelia and the milkman liked one another. They often talked together in the kitchen. And Amelia never seemed that happy at school with Miss Minchin always bossing her around. Sara leaned further out the window, lost in thought.

Suddenly Sara heard Miss Minchin's angry voice behind her. "Where is it?" Miss Minchin asked. "Where is the locket?"

Sara whirled around. She touched her locket around her neck.

"Give it to me!" Miss Minchin said as she advanced toward Sara. Tearfully, Sara removed the locket. Miss Minchin grabbed it out of her hands. Then she stared in shock at Sara's changed room.

"What is all this?" she asked Sara. "Where did it come from?"

"I . . . I don't know," Sara answered. "I just woke up and it was here."

"You stole all of it, didn't you? Just like you stole this locket!"

"No!" Sara protested.

Miss Minchin narrowed her small eyes. "You're nothing but a dirty little thief," she said.

"Miss Minchin — " Sara pleaded.

"Pack your things," Miss Minchin interrupted. "You'll be leaving with the police very shortly."

Sara was too terrified to say anything more. Miss Minchin left the room and slammed the door behind her.

Sara banged on her door, but Miss Minchin had locked her in. "Please!" she said, sobbing. "I didn't do it!"

Downstairs, Miss Minchin called the police. "You heard me. I want her picked up immediately," she said into the phone. She looked at Sara's locket and threw it angrily against the wall. It opened. . . .

Clouds began to cover the full moon. The wind gusted. Thunder rumbled overhead. Rain pelted against the windows.

Sara lay down on her bed and cried and cried. Becky tried to comfort her. "I'm sure they'll believe you," Becky said.

"No," Sara's voice sounded muffled. "I have to get away."

"But how?" Becky asked. "My room's locked, too."

Just then, the girls heard a wagon pull up in front of the school. "The police, they're here!" Becky said from the window.

Sara looked outside. Her heart sank when she saw that the wooden plank connecting her room with the one next door was missing.

Quickly, Sara took one of the wooden slats from under her mattress. With Becky's help, she put the board on her windowsill. It stretched across to Ram Dass's.

Miss Minchin ushered the two policemen inside. She led them up the attic stairs.

Sara climbed out the window onto the unsteady board. The rain poured down, making the wood slippery.

"Sara, you'll fall!" Becky said.

"I can do it," Sara said. She turned to give Becky one last hug. "I'll come back for you," she promised.

Sara began her walk across the board while Hanuman watched her. At that moment, Miss Minchin burst into Sara's room with the two policemen. She saw Becky by the open window and leaned outside.

"What are you doing?" she called to Sara. "Come back here this instant!" She reached out to grab the hem of Sara's dress. Sara stumbled — and almost fell off — the slippery board. She regained her balance and began to crawl. Miss Minchin lost her grip.

"The little beast is running away!" Miss Minchin shouted. Suddenly a clap of thunder shook the building. A gutter fell from the roof and snapped the board in half.

"Sara!" Becky screamed.

Sara managed to grab Ram Dass's windowsill. She dangled by her fingertips over the alleyway, far below. Becky, Miss Minchin, and the policemen watched in horror.

Sara took a deep breath. Slowly, she managed to pull herself up. Hanuman waited for her to come inside before he jumped in her arms.

"Well, don't just stand there," Miss Minchin told the policemen angrily. "Go next door and find her!"

20

Sara could not believe she was really in Mr. Randolph's house. But she wasn't safe yet. Quietly, she sneaked down the big staircase. Hanuman followed her.

On the ground floor of the brownstone, Sara heard muffled voices coming from the study.

Mr. Randolph sat by the fire talking with the wounded soldier. The soldier no longer had bandages on his eyes. He could now see.

"It's just the not knowing that's so painful," Mr. Randolph said. "I can't let go of John until I find out what happened."

"I'm sorry. I wish I could help you," the soldier said.

Sara tiptoed past the open door of the study. Hanuman walked silently behind her. The two men did not notice.

"You sound as though you've experienced such a loss," Mr. Randolph continued.

The wounded soldier nodded. "It's strange — feeling your heart remember something your mind cannot," he said.

By now Sara was at the front door. She reached for the knob just as Miss Minchin and the two policemen banged on the door from outside. Sara dashed into the living room, closing the sliding doors behind her.

"Who can that be at this hour?" Mr. Randolph asked. Ram Dass left the study to go answer the door.

"I'm sorry to bother you, but a child from the school has escaped into your house," Miss Minchin told Ram Dass.

"Ram Dass, what is going on here?" Mr. Randolph asked as he wheeled his chair into the front hall.

"There is a child hiding in this house unlawfully," Miss Minchin answered.

"What?" Mr. Randolph exclaimed.

The policemen then took charge. One policeman searched the upstairs while the other headed right for the living room door.

Sara heard the policeman's heavy footsteps approach. Quickly, she opened another set of sliding doors that led from the living room to the study. If

72

Sara had not been so scared, she would have marveled at what a wonderful house this was.

Suddenly a bolt of lightning struck. It left the house in complete darkness.

"What now?!" Mr. Randolph exclaimed. "Ram Dass, bring some candles!"

As the policeman came in the living room, Sara tiptoed into the study. The wounded soldier sat in the shadows. He heard Sara come in, but he could not see her.

"Who's there?" he called.

Sara had not been expecting anyone in the study. She was so scared she began to cry.

"I won't hurt you," the wounded soldier said as he came toward Sara. "Won't you tell me your name?"

The room was so dark, Sara couldn't see the soldier's face. "Sara," she answered, whimpering.

"Sara," the wounded soldier repeated. "That's such a pretty name," he said as he stepped into the light cast by the fire in the fireplace.

For the first time, Sara saw the soldier's face. She stared and stared as if she were looking at a ghost. Slowly, she rose from the floor.

"Papa . . ." she said.

"What? What did you say?" Captain Crewe answered.

Sara threw her arms around his legs and hugged him. "Papa," she repeated. "Papa, it's me. . . . It's Sara!"

Captain Crewe looked very confused. He knelt before the little girl. "Sara, do you know me?" he asked.

"Oh, Papa, don't you remember me?" Sara sounded heartbroken. She heard footsteps and voices outside the room.

Captain Crewe tried. "I can't seem to remember," he said, shaking his head.

At that moment, Miss Minchin burst into the room with the policemen. Mr. Randolph wheeled himself in, followed by Ram Dass.

"Sara!" Miss Minchin exclaimed.

"Papa, please!" Sara pleaded. Miss Minchin turned to the wounded soldier. She recognized Captain Crewe and went very pale.

"Do you know this man?" Mr. Randolph asked Sara.

"Papa, tell them!"

Miss Minchin noticed Captain Crewe's blank look. Quickly, she turned to the police. "This child has no father. Take her away."

"No, no," Sara sobbed. Captain Crewe looked on helplessly as the police began to drag Sara out of the room.

"Papa, please! You must know me," Sara sobbed, struggling to escape. *"It's Sara!"* The police pulled her out of the room. Miss Minchin and Mr. Randolph followed.

"Remember?! Remember India!? And Maya? And mean Clara Pideson?" Sara cried.

21

Miss Minchin and the police led Sara to the waiting police wagon. Sara still struggled to free herself. She cried as if her heart were breaking.

Captain Crewe dashed outside. Sara's cries had stirred his memory and he began to run after her.

"Sara!" Captain Crewe shouted as he raced toward the wagon. Sara broke free and rushed into her father's arms.

"Oh, my darling. My darling Sara," her father said, kissing her.

"Oh, Papa, you're back. You're back!" Sara shouted.

Miss Minchin watched them. She looked furious. She turned away and saw the policemen looking at her with raised eyebrows. She knew she was in trouble.

Two months later, many things had changed. Miss Minchin's Seminary was now called The Randolph School for Girls. Miss Minchin had been allowed to stay on, but she now worked as a chimney sweep.

Mr. Randolph sat outside in his wheelchair watching the school girls play a ball game in the park. Ram Dass and Hanuman were beside him.

Soon a carriage pulled up at the curb. Captain Crewe stepped outside and held the door open for Sara and Becky. All three were beautifully dressed.

"All ready for your trip?" Mr. Randolph greeted them.

Captain Crewe nodded. "I can't thank you enough, Mr. Randolph, for everything you've done."

Mr. Randolph smiled warmly. "No more than what you tried to do for my son," he said.

Captain Crewe gave the elderly man a sympathetic look.

"Take care, Mr. Randolph," said Captain Crewe.

"You too," Mr. Randolph answered. "Must be good to be going home to India."

Captain Crewe looked at Ram Dass and nodded.

Ram Dass smiled at him.

* * *

Ermengarde, Betsy, Gertrude, and Lottie left the ball game to say good-bye to Sara and Becky. Sara was holding Emily. "I have a surprise for you all," she said as she handed the doll to Lottie.

"Emily!" Lottie shrieked in surprise.

"Whenever you think of me just tell Emily and she'll get the message to me," Sara said. "And when you hug her, you'll really be getting a hug from me."

"Then we'll hug her every day," said Ermengarde.

Many weeks later, Captain Crewe, Sara, and Becky stood on the deck of the ship. They could see the Himalayas in the distance, welcoming them with open arms.

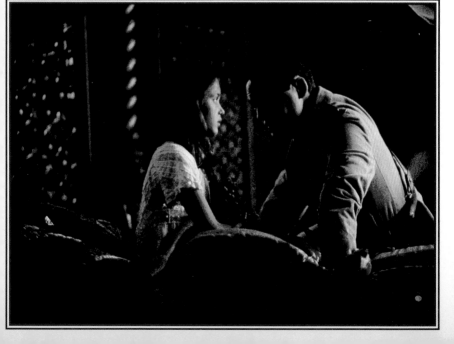

~♥~

---❤---